Christmas Wonderland

Illustrated by Gill Guile
Text by Gill Davies

Brown Watson
ENGLAND

Contents

First published 2006 by Brown Watson
The Old Mill, 76 Fleckney Road
Kibworth Beauchamp, Leics LE8 0HG

ISBN: 978-0-7097-1735-5
© 2006 Brown Watson
Reprinted 2007
Printed in China

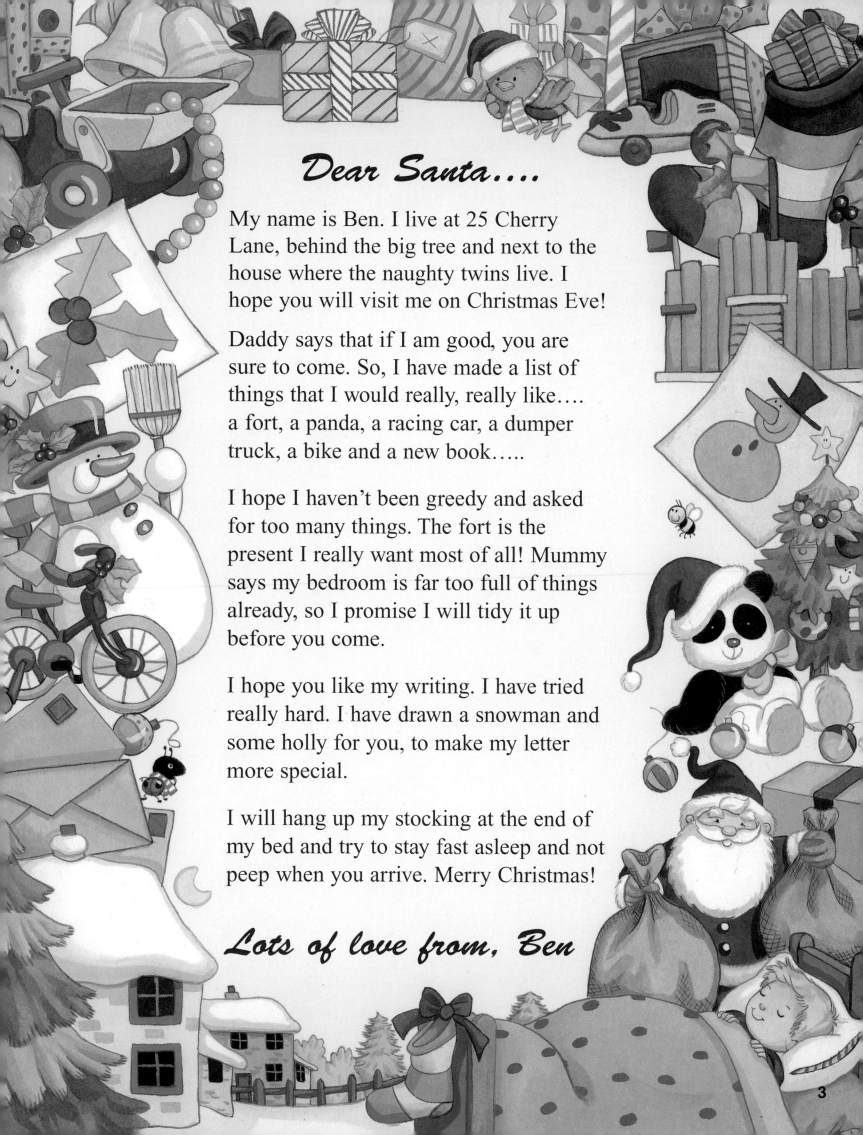

Dear Santa....

My name is Ben. I live at 25 Cherry Lane, behind the big tree and next to the house where the naughty twins live. I hope you will visit me on Christmas Eve!

Daddy says that if I am good, you are sure to come. So, I have made a list of things that I would really, really like…. a fort, a panda, a racing car, a dumper truck, a bike and a new book…..

I hope I haven't been greedy and asked for too many things. The fort is the present I really want most of all! Mummy says my bedroom is far too full of things already, so I promise I will tidy it up before you come.

I hope you like my writing. I have tried really hard. I have drawn a snowman and some holly for you, to make my letter more special.

I will hang up my stocking at the end of my bed and try to stay fast asleep and not peep when you arrive. Merry Christmas!

Lots of love from, Ben

The Sleepy Elf

It is very busy in Toyland. The elves are working very, very hard. Some are making toys. Some are polishing the sleigh. Others are rushing to collect the latest batch of letters for Father Christmas. Yet more elves are sorting through the lists of all the toys that will soon be needed.

Sonny Elf is very, very tired. He has been making wooden trains and sledges and wagons full of bricks and now his head hurts from all the banging noises in the workshop. His little fingers are sore from the hammering of nails. And his legs ache from running around to fetch things.

Sonny puts his head down on the workbench to rest for just a moment . . . and soon he is fast asleep.

The other elves giggle and point but they are very kind so they tiptoe around him as Sonny sleeps on, dreaming of summer when he can play hide and seek with the polar bears.

Soon Father Christmas arrives. He laughs when he sees Sonny sleeping, then scoops him up and carries Sonny back to his tiny elf bed in his tiny little log cabin.

"I have been working everyone too hard," says Father Christmas to all the elves. "Let's have a holiday today."

So all the elves rush out to play in the snow and toboggan or to ride the reindeer. Then they go home to sit in their snug armchairs and read books or do puzzles.

When Sonny wakes up he is very surprised to find himself in bed and even more surprised to see the other elves playing outside and waving to him through the window.

"You have done us all a good turn," they call out. "Today is a holiday because of you!"

The next day all the elves go back to their Christmas work, feeling refreshed and happy. And from that year onwards, they always have a day's holiday before the final Christmas rush.

Little Donkey

Little Donkey is tired. He has been plodding along for hours now, up and down hills, past big boulders and lonely shepherd huts, ever on along the hard stony road.

His legs hurt. His back aches. But still he keeps going, one little weary hoof after another: clip, clop... clip, clop... clip, clop.

At last he can see Bethlehem. The lights are twinkling in the little town below them, nestling in the hills.

Mary leans over and strokes his head. "Thank you, Donkey," she whispers. "We are nearly there. Soon you can rest."

Her voice is so warm and soft that Donkey forgets he is tired. He forgets the hard, stony path. He almost gallops into Bethlehem.

Somehow Donkey knows that this is a very special night. Something wonderful is going to happen, although he cannot guess what this might be.

At last they are in the middle of town, but still there is no chance to rest. They push their way through the busy streets but all the places they hope to stay are full to overflowing.

"No room! No room!" says one innkeeper after another.

"Poor Donkey," says Mary, patting his head. "You must be such a tired old thing by now. Let me just slip off and walk for a while, so you can catch your breath."

Then Donkey spots the stable. It looks very warm and cosy. Donkey whinnies and nudges Joseph to show him that here at last is somewhere to stay.

"Oh-ho," laughs the innkeeper. "Now that's an idea, old fellow. Your owners can share the stable with you, if you like. There's plenty of room in there."

Later that night, Donkey wakes. The stable is lit by the most brilliant star he has ever seen and Mary has given birth to a baby boy. Mary gently places the tiny child to sleep in the soft hay, right next to Donkey. So Donkey stays wide awake and watches over the new baby in his manger all night.

Angels sing in the night sky and shepherds and three wise men arrive to visit Jesus and to give him wonderful presents. "Hee-Haw!" Donkey whispers, "I am so happy you have been born tonight. I shall take good care of you."

Then Donkey sighs and grins as the baby gurgles and seems to reach up to touch his soft furry nose. What a wonderful night this has been.

Happy Christmas!

The fairy on the Christmas tree had a little, silver wand, wore a crown of pearls and tiny gems and a pretty lace dress. "You look so beautiful," sighed all the other decorations on the tree.

But the fairy did not smile. Although she was, indeed, quite beautiful, she was very unhappy. Big tears rolled down her pretty pink cheeks. "Whatever is the matter?" asked the bells and the balls and the garlands.

"I am lonely," cried the sad little fairy. "There are lots of you, but there is only one of me. I need another fairy to talk to now and then." At that very moment a little girl ran into the room to see the wonderful Christmas tree.

"Oh, it is beautiful," she cried, clapping her hands in delight. Then her face changed and she looked a little sad. "But where is my lovely old fairy?" she asked.

17

"We have bought a fine new one," her father explained. "Oh, she is very pretty," said the little girl. "But I do love our old fairy and would be very sad if she had to stay in a box in the attic and not enjoy Christmas with us."

So Mother rushed upstairs and found the old fairy and the little girl grinned as Father put the old fairy on top of the tree next to the new one. "Now we have two beautiful fairies on our tree!" squealed the little girl, dancing up and down. "Aren't we lucky!"

The new little fairy smiled now and was as happy as can be. . . and the old fairy was happy too, to be rescued from the attic and thrilled to bits to find a new friend waiting for her.

When the family closed the door that night, the two fairies danced on the top of the tree while all the decorations shimmered with delight. What a happy Christmas they all had!

The Giant Snowball

"Let's make snowballs," suggested Rascal
Rabbit one Christmas Eve.
"Let's make the biggest in the forest," laughed Pixie.
"Let's make the biggest in the land," giggled Rolypoly.
"Let's make the biggest snowball in the world,"
shrieked Pickles.

So the rabbits set about rolling a snowball. At first it
was just the size of their paws, then their heads and
then it was as high as the little rabbits stood.

"That's big," said Rascal.
"But not the biggest in the forest," said Rolypoly.
"Nor the land," laughed Pixie.
"Nor the world," shrieked Pickles.

"Why don't we roll it down the hill," suggested Rascal.

So they did. The snowball rolled slowly at first,
then faster and faster, picking up snow and growing
bigger as it went. Soon it was ENORMOUS! The
giant snowball rolled down into the village. Everyone
came out to stare as it thundered past, narrowly missing
the post squirrel on his bike and a party of carol-singing
kittens. It rolled onto the frozen pond, scattering the ducks.

The icc cracked. The huge snowball bobbed about and
then began to melt.

"That was a wonderful splash," laughed Rascal Rabbit.
"The biggest splash in the forest," laughed Rolypoly.
"The biggest in the land," giggled Pixie.
"That was the biggest splash in all the world!" shrieked Pickles.

Then the happy rabbits went home
to hang up their stockings.

Grandpa's Christmas Day

"There is a Grandpa here who would like a skateboard," laughs Santa Claus as he opens the Christmas mail.

There are all sorts of Grandpas. Some tell jokes, some smoke pipes or eat toffees or do crossword puzzles. Lots of them go to sleep and snore all afternoon. But this Grandpa is different. He doesn't want to be an old-fashioned, grown-up Grandpa.

"He hasn't asked for anything sensible, like a pair of slippers or a handkerchief," Santa Claus tells the reindeer. "He would like a bright orange jacket and a skateboard."

Santa Claus is surprised but he tells the elves, "I shall be very happy to help."

On Christmas Eve, Grandpa joins his grandchildren and hangs up his stocking, too. When Santa Claus arrives with the presents, he laughs and tells the reindeer, "He looks just like me!"

24

The next morning Grandpa is thrilled to see that his stocking is bulging with toffees and books, a blue bobble hat and scarf, the shiny orange jacket he wanted and a wonderful purple and silver skateboard.

Grandpa is very excited. He puts on the new clothes and sets off to try out the skateboard.

"Off I go!" says Grandpa, as the grandchildren stare in amazement and run out into the street to watch. "I've been longing to try one of these scraper-board thingummies," Grandpa tells them all, grinning from ear to ear.

Luckily, as it is Christmas Day, there are not too many cars around as Grandpa wobbles about . . . and crashes into the icicles on the hedge . . . and falls off . . . but soon he has the hang of it.

He has a wonderful Christmas morning. When you are very grown up, it is easy to forget how exciting it feels to swish along with the wind whistling past your ears, because you haven't done that sort of thing for a long while.

Soon Grandpa is feeling tired and hungry. So he races home to join the family for lunch. He sits down to read one of his new books and, in no time at all, he falls fast asleep.

"He looks like an ordinary Grandpa now," say his grandchildren, but they know he isn't really.

The Most Important Night

Little Angel was puzzled. Normally Heaven was such a quiet, peaceful place but today all the angels were flying around in a whirl.

"What is happening?" asked Little Angel. "No time to talk now, I'll explain later just as soon as I have a moment to pause," promised Great Uncle Gabriel, hurrying past.

Some angels were tuning their harps; some were polishing their halos; some were flying high to give their wings a good workout. Their best angel robes had been washed and were hanging on fluffy white clouds to dry.

Meanwhile, Little Angel could hear the choir practising their beautiful singing. Everyone in heaven was very, very busy all day . . ..

Then, as evening came, they flew out through the Gates of Heaven, leaving Little Angel sitting all on her own.

"Phew! What a day!" sighed the White Dove, flying down to perch beside Little Angel. "I thought they'd never be ready for the Most Important Night."

"What is going on?" asked puzzled Little Angel.

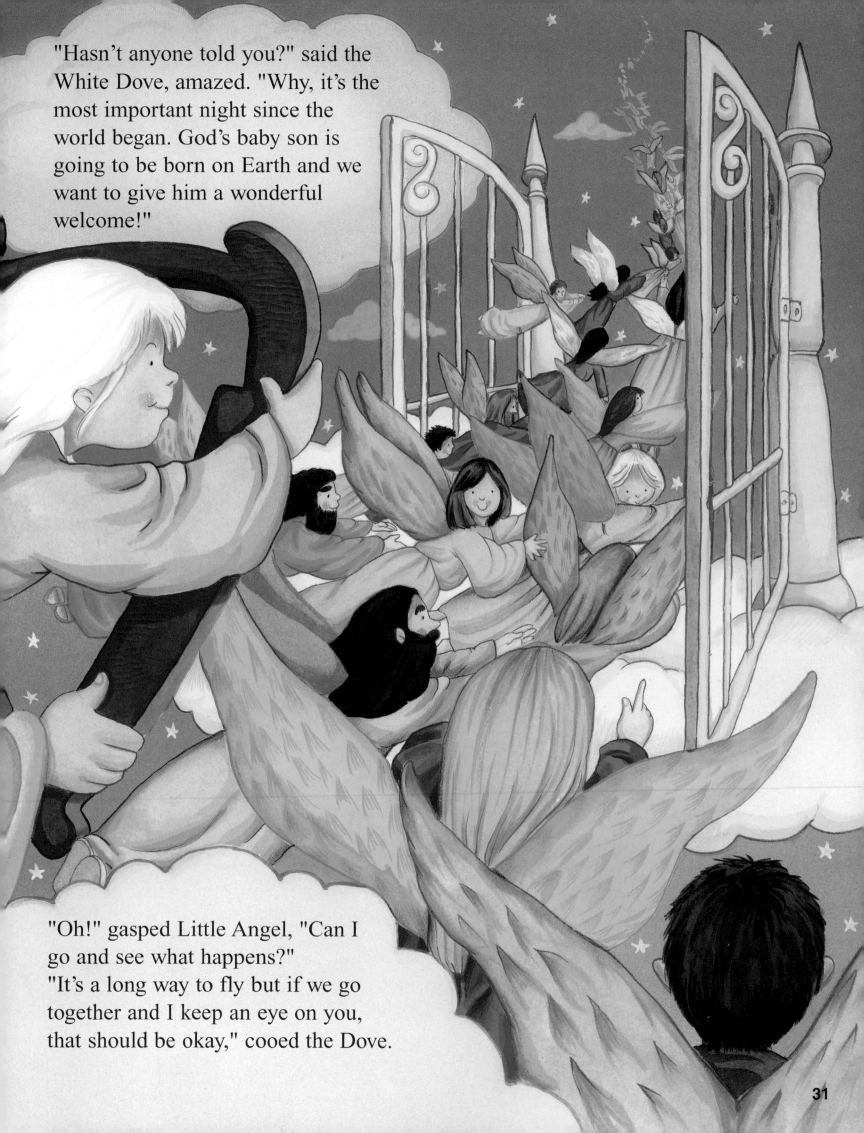

"Hasn't anyone told you?" said the White Dove, amazed. "Why, it's the most important night since the world began. God's baby son is going to be born on Earth and we want to give him a wonderful welcome!"

"Oh!" gasped Little Angel, "Can I go and see what happens?"
"It's a long way to fly but if we go together and I keep an eye on you, that should be okay," cooed the Dove.

Off they flew into the beautiful dark night. All the stars were gleaming brightly and they found the angel choir singing above a stable lit by a brilliant star. There inside lay baby Jesus.

Little Angel pulled out one of her beautiful gold-tipped feathers and gave it to the baby. He clutched the feather in his little fist and gazed up at Little Angel.

"Thank you," said the baby's mother and, as she smiled while the baby gurgled happily, Little Angel was no longer puzzled. Somehow she knew that this baby was very special and that tonight really was the Most Important Night ever..